WOLFIE

Written by Jonathan Shipton
&
Illustrated by Jenny Williams

Albury Books

For Archie, Stella, Arlo, Arthur and Nerys. J.C.S.

For Juniper and Eden. J.W.

This edition published in 2018
by Albury Books

Albury Court, Albury, Thame,
Oxfordshire, OX9 2LP
United Kingdom

www.AlburyBooks.com

ISBN 978-1-910571-61-3

A CIP catalogue record for this title is available from the British Library

Printed and bound in China

Not so very long ago,
on the other side of the woods,
there was a little girl,
    and there was also a...

Now, this wolf was a little bit different, because he didn't eat people. Not even a teeny tiny nibble.

But nobody believed him.

Instead, they took one look at his great big feet and sharp white teeth and ran away SCREAMING!

All Wolfie wanted to do was play, but every time he tried to join in, people shouted and threw rocks at him. They really hurt!

So Wolfie gave up trying to join in.

He sloped away over the hills,
through the deep woods,
up the stony mountain side,
back to his dark and lonely cave...

Where he
howled himself
to sleep.

Meanwhile, the little girl was busy helping her mum out on their farm.

She counted the chickens...

And she climbed the trees in the orchard to pick the ripest apples.

There was always lots to do on the farm.

One day, the little girl
was looking for blackberries.
She searched and searched, but
she couldn't find any!

She decided to walk a little bit
further, but she didn't tell her mum,
because it was only supposed to be
a short walk...

Before long, the little girl
was at the edge of the woods.

She was never, ever allowed to
go in to the woods on her own,
but she could see some BIG, FAT, JUICY
blackberries just ahead of her...

and they tasted
DELICIOUS!

A bit further on,
she spotted some nuts...

and then a butterfly.

There were so
many interesting
things to see!

Before long,
the little girl had wondered
quite deep in to the woods.

The trees all started to look
very similar, and the little
girl wasn't quite sure which
way she'd come from.

The sun was going down and the forest was starting to get dark...

And although she tried to be brave, the little girl felt a bit scared.

Quietly, she began to cry.

Wolfie slid and scrambled down the mountainside,

splashed through the stream,

and galloped through the leaves.

finally, with one enormous

LEAP!

Wolfie landed right in front of the little girl,

who was so surprised,
she stopped crying at once.

Wolfie looked at the little girl.

The little girl looked at Wolfie.

Wolfie waited for the little girl to scream.

The little girl waited for Wolfie to

EAT HER UP!

But nothing happened...

In fact, this wolf looked quite friendly.

So, very slowly she reached out her hand,
and very gently she stroked Wolfie's head.

Wolfie had never been
stroked before.

He was so
delighted that he bounded
straight in to a great big pile
of leaves and rolled round and round.

The little girl laughed at how silly he looked.

Then Wolfie jumped up and
started chasing his tail round
and round in a circle.
And the more he chased,
the more the little girl laughed!

She completely forgot
about being lost,
until suddenly
an owl flew past.

Hoooo Hoooo Hooo

The little girl stopped laughing.

She wanted to go home.

But she still didn't know how.

Wolfie really wanted to help, but he was scared.

He didn't want people to throw big rocks at him again.
He didn't want people to scream and shout at him again.

Wolfie knew he was going to have to be REALLY brave if he was going to help his new friend.

Wolfie helped the little girl jump on
his back, and by the light of
the moon they bounded
back through
the woods.

They jumped
over rocks, they splashed
through the stream, they twisted
past brambles, and galloped
through leaves until...

finally they arrived safe
and sound back at the farm,
where the little girl's mum was
waiting to give her a GREAT BIG HUG.

Poor Wolfie
was very sad.

He didn't eat people.
He didn't even bite.

But nobody believed him...

Well, nobody except the little girl.

(and maybe the little girl's mum!)